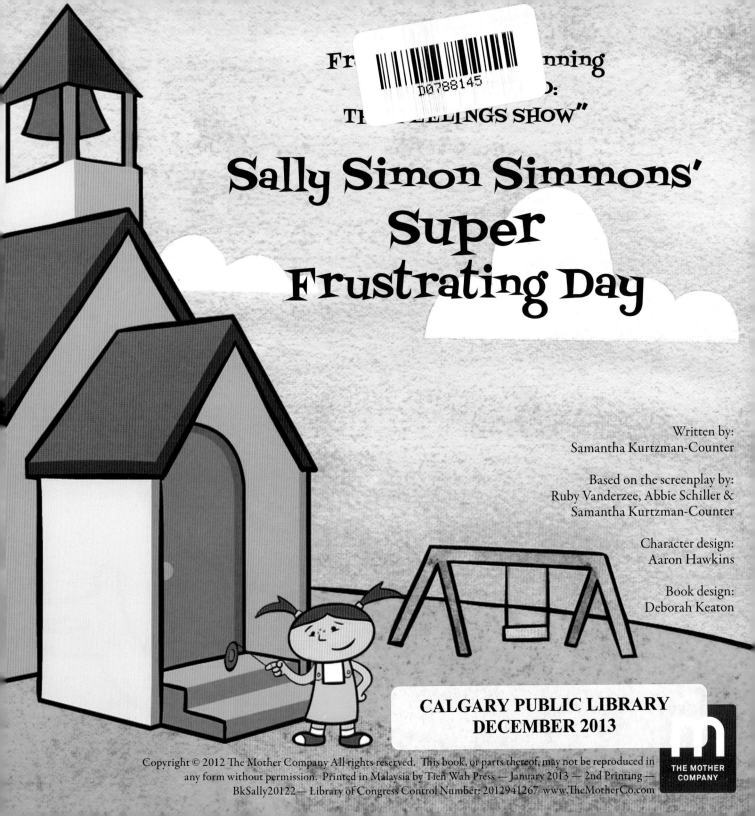

From the Emmy Award winning series:
"Ruby's Studio: THE FEELINGS SHOW"

Sally Simon Simmons'
Super Frustrating Day

Written by:
Samantha Kurtzman-Counter

Based on the screenplay by:
Ruby Vanderzee, Abbie Schiller &
Samantha Kurtzman-Counter

Character design:
Aaron Hawkins

Book design:
Deborah Keaton

THE MOTHER COMPANY

One day at Sally's school there was a project just her style...

"It's double-decker sandwich day...Let's make one stretch a mile!"

"A double-decker sandwich?
Yessirreee, let's get down to it!
Mine is going to touch the sky!"
She knew that
she could do it!

Sally built that
SANDWICH fast,
layer after layer:
lettuce, pickles,
mustard, cheese,
each went on
with care -
lettuce, pickles,
mustard, cheese,
rose high INTO
THE AIR!

Sally kept on piling,
and her sandwich
got too tall-
"**Wibble-Wobble-Tilt!**"
it went -and soon
began to fall!

What an awful mess I've made - who knew that mustard flies?!

Sally sat and thought:
"This time I have to make it stick-
I'll pile it even faster now.
That ought to do the trick!"

so Sally started fresh;
she was determined not to stop.

Sally Simon Simmons'
face was red
and fiery hot.
She ducked to hide
behind the mess,
happy she was not.

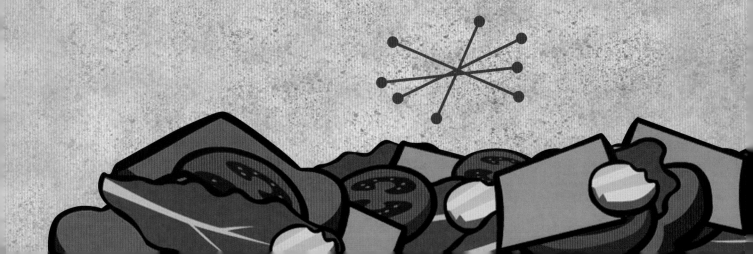

The **teacher** turned
and saw Sally's frustration
grow and grow.
He knew that her big feelings
meant some tears
might start to flow.

"I wanted mine
to touch the Sky!"
The teacher heard her cry...

Sally Simon Simmons set her frustration aside – she sat right down, took a deep breath and then again she **tried.**

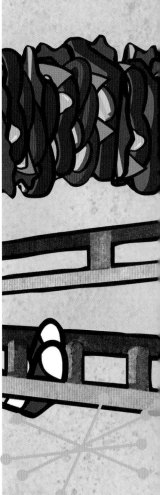

She worked her way so slowly,
from the bottom to the top.

She took her time, made sure it stuck-
they thought she'd never stop!

Just as **Sally** made the move to set
the final bread, the tower began to wobble.
Would it fall and crash instead?

But Sally knew just what to do:
"I'll breathe and take it slow!
And if it falls, I did my best-
and that's the way to go!"

"It's the **tallest**, super duperest sandwich in the **world!**"

Boys and girls, remember
Sally Simon Simmons' success:
Work through your own
frustration and
just try to do your best.

A Note to Parents and Teachers

Helping children develop a basic understanding of their feelings is one of our most important jobs as parents and educators. When children are able to access, understand, and express what they feel, they sail more smoothly through their days, playing, socializing and cooperating.

Frustration is an intense experience for young children. Parenting experts advise allowing children to feel their frustration and learn to move through it, rather than making it go away or trying to avoid it altogether. This skill builds resilience and character that help children navigate their lives for years to come.

Research shows that supporting emotional literacy in children before age five sets them up for more success in school, in relationships, and in life. It is our goal at The Mother Company to present children with beautiful, engaging products that offer them the words and skills to become more self-aware, communicative, and cooperative. Our motto is "Helping Parents Raise Good People." We hope you find this book to be one step closer to reaching that goal.

– Abbie Schiller & Sam Kurtzman-Counter, The Mother Company Mamas

Guided by the mission to "Help Parents Raise Good People," The Mother Company offers world-renowned expert advice for parents at TheMotherCo.com, as well as the "Ruby's Studio" line of award-winning products for children.

THE MOTHER COMPANY

Hi, I'm Ruby! What's your name?

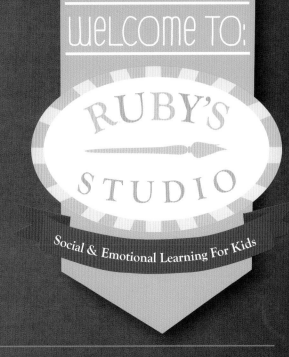

WELCOME TO:

RUBY'S STUDIO

Social & Emotional Learning For Kids

RUBY'S STUDIO is a line of HELPFUL, FUN, AWARD-WINNING PRODUCTS designed to enhance communication, cooperation, and self-understanding in young children.

Videos

Toys & Activities

Mobile Apps & eBooks

Music

Enriching Books

Helping Parents Raise Good People:
RubysStudio.com

NATIONAL WINNER PARENTING AWARDS

The Mother Company Presents

RUBY'S STUDIO

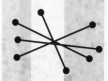
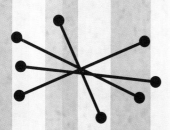

Social & Emotional Learning For Kids

www.RubysStudio.com